The Sun, the Moon, and the Gardener's Son

By Charles Heilbronn

Illustrations by Y. Z. Kami

HARRY N. ABRAMS, INC., PUBLISHERS

As they did every morning, the Big
Blue Sky, the Little Black Cloud, the Earth,
the Moon, and the Gardener waited
for the Sun to rise.

Cockadoodle-doo!
Cockadoodle-doo!

As it did every morning, the Rooster crowed.

As he did every morning, the
Gardener went to wake his Son.
But this morning, something was
different.

"It's still dark!" cried the Gardener's Son.

"Yes," replied the Gardener. "The
Rooster crowed, but the Sun has not
risen and the colors do not sparkle over
the Universe. I hope the Sun is
not sick."

Everyone was very worried.

So the Gardener, his Son, the Big Blue Sky, the Little Black Cloud, and the Earth went in search of the Sun.

The Moon did not join them. She had to shine while the Sun was still missing even though her meager light did not make the colors of the Universe dance.

At last the Sun was found.

He was still asleep, but hearing their approach, he slowly opened his eyes.

"I know why you have come, but you shouldn't have bothered," the Sun told them. "I'm not getting up this morning."

"Why?" the Gardener's Son asked kindly.

"Last night, the Moon passed in front of me! She eclipsed me without a word, a smile, a look. It was like I didn't exist! I have made up my mind: I will not rise this morning and, perhaps, tomorrow morning and the morning after that and the morning after that.

"This will serve the Moon right! She will have to work day and night forever!

"I will no longer shine, and the colors of the Universe will be miserable, lifeless, and without a smile."

And so that morning, the Sun refused to rise and the colors of the Universe remained dull, cast in the Moon's dim glow.

On that same morning, there was a little flower, a most handsome little poppy. When Poppy heard that the Sun might never rise again, he started to cry. "Yesterday, I was warm and happy and growing swiftly under the colors of the Sun.

"Today I am cold and afraid. Without the Sun's light, I may lose my beautiful red petals."

Hearing his sobs, the Gardener's Son approached Poppy to try and comfort him.

Slowly, very slowly, he poured water on Poppy's red petals and whispered the sweetest words he knew.

"Ahh-ahh-CHOO," sneezed the Poppy. "Your water is so cold! Do you really think the Sun will never rise again? Will the Universe stay cold, dark, and without colors?"

The Gardener's Son did not want to answer. He kneeled silently next to the Poppy and dug some dirt to keep the flower warm.

Meanwhile, the Gardener was very worried.

He walked and walked and walked and finally returned to stare at the giant cloud, behind which the Sun was hiding.

Suddenly, out of the dark,
cold, sad, colorless morning,
a pixie appeared!
 She saw how nice the
Gardener's Son was to Poppy.
 "You are so kind," she said.

The pixie was so small, she stood on Poppy's petals.

"Who are you?" asked the Gardener's Son.

"I am a pixie. My name is Rainbow," she said. "I paint in the dark."

The Gardener's Son said, "What do you paint?"

Rainbow said, "Watch!"

Rainbow slowly shut her big blue eyes and the Universe
started rocking....
The Big Blue Sky turned purple.
The Little Black Cloud turned purple.
The watering can turned purple.

The Poppy turned purple.

All the plants turned purple.

Even the Gardener's Son turned purple.

"How strange," said the Gardener's Son. "How do you do it?"

"Easy," said Rainbow. "I paint with my eyes. Watch!"

Once again, Rainbow slowly shut her big blue eyes and the Universe started rocking even harder....

The Big Blue Sky turned green.

The Little Black Cloud turned green.

The watering can turned green.

The Poppy turned green.

All the plants turned green.

And the Gardener's Son turned green, too!

"Again!" giggled the Gardener's Son.

Rainbow, once more, closed her big blue eyes and
everything turned orange and rocked even more....
The Big Blue Sky turned orange.
The Little Black Cloud turned orange.
The watering can turned orange.

The Poppy turned orange.

All the plants turned orange.

And the Gardener's Son turned orange!

As the colors changed over the Universe, the Sun
and the Moon saw what Rainbow was showing the
Gardener's Son: a world of colors brimming, teeming,
and bubbling with laughter and life.

The Moon could not allow the Universe to be
colorless. The Universe needed the Sun to shine.
The Moon apologized to the Sun for snubbing him.

The Sun, realizing how selfish he had been,
immediately accepted the Moon's apology. He
emerged from his blanket of clouds and shone as
hard as he could.

As the Universe suddenly lit up and all the colors reappeared, Poppy, the little poppy, had disappeared and in his place that morning, unlike other mornings, was Coccinelle, a little polka-dotted turtle that came out of nowhere.

FOR MY FATHER AND MY MOTHER,
who knew well Coccinelle,
the little polka-dotted turtle.

—C. H.

Coccimelle, la petite tortue à pois

DESIGN COORDINATOR, ENGLISH-LANGUAGE EDITION: Darilyn Lowe Carnes

Library of Congress Cataloging-in-Publication Data

Heilbronn, Charles.
  [Arroseur de l'univers. English]
  The sun, the moon, and the gardener's son / by Charles Heilbronn;
illustrated by Y.Z. Kami.
      p. cm.
Summary: The gardener's son and Rainbow, who can change the color of
things, do what they can to help when the Moon and the Sun quarrel.
  ISBN 0-8109-5025-1
  [1. Sun—Fiction. 2. Moon—Fiction. 3. Color—Fiction.
4.Gardening—Fiction.] I. Kami, Y. Z., ill. II. Title.
  PZ7.H3665 Gar 2001
  [E]—dc21   00-056554

Copyright © 1999 De La Martinière Jeunesse
English translation copyright © 2001 Harry N. Abrams, Inc.

Printed and bound in Belgium

 Harry N. Abrams, Inc.
100 Fifth Avenue
New York, N.Y. 10011
www.abramsbooks.com